STAR TREK

Fun with
Kirk and Spock

A Parody

Robb Pearlman

CIDER MILL PRESS

BOOK PUBLISHERS

Fun with Kirk and Spock: A Parody

STARTREK.COM™

This is an officially licensed book by Cider Mill Press Book Publishers LLC.

13-Digit ISBN: 978-1-60433-476-0
10-Digit ISBN: 1-60433-476-2

This book may be ordered by mail from the publisher.
Please include $5.99 for postage and handling.
Please support your local bookseller first!

Books published by Cider Mill Press Book Publishers are available at special discounts
for bulk purchases in the United States by corporations, institutions, and other organizations.
For more information, please contact the publisher.

Cider Mill Press Book Publishers
"Where good books are ready for press"
501 Nelson Place
Nashville, Tennessee 37214

cidermillpress.com

Design by Tango Media
Illustrations by Gary Shipman

Printed in Malaysia
24 25 26 27 28 COS 12 11 10 9 8

See the *Enterprise*.
See the *Enterprise* go boldly.
Go go go, *Enterprise*!
Go boldly!

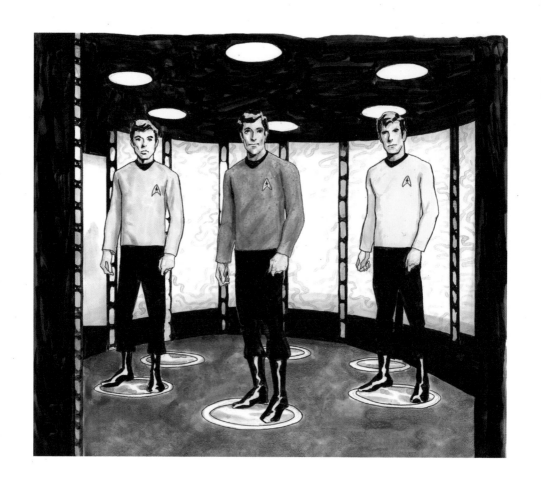

Three crew members beam down
to a mysterious planet.
One Red shirt. One Blue shirt.
One Yellow shirt.
Three crew members beam down.
Three crew members have an adventure.

Two crew members beam back up
to the *Enterprise*.

One Blue shirt. One Yellow shirt.

Two crew members beam back up.

One crew member is fondly remembered.

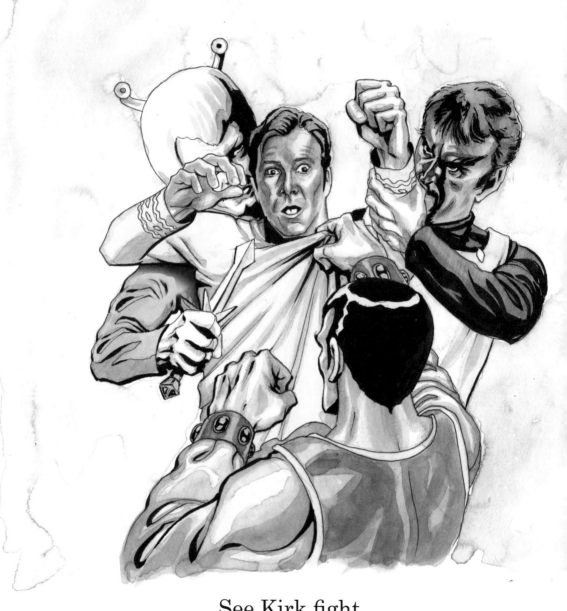

See Kirk fight.

Fight, Kirk, fight!

Kirk is outnumbered.

Kirk is hurt.

Kirk wins!

Kirk knows a chop to the neck
will do the trick every time.

See Spock.
See Spock push down
his feelings.
Down, down, down!
Push push push.
No one smiles on Vulcan.

See Spock.

See Spock raise his hand for the traditional Vulcan greeting.

"Live long and prosper," says Spock.

See the Ensign.

See the Ensign try to get his fingers to cooperate.

A Jefferies tube is good for many things.
A Jefferies tube is good for climbing
from one deck to another.
A Jefferies tube is good for finding ways
to stop the M-5 from taking over the ship.
A Jefferies tube is good for housing
a matter-antimatter reaction chamber.
A Jefferies tube is *not* good for hiding
a dead Tellarite.

The captain and his crew work on the bridge.
The bridge is safe and secure.
Nobody bad is allowed on the bridge.
Except murderous children controlled by a megalomaniacal noncorporeal entity.
And conniving Romulan commanders.
And inquisitive Klingon science officers.
And psychotic satellites.
Otherwise, the bridge is safe and secure.

See Nurse Chapel.
Nurse Chapel made soup
for Spock.
It is good soup, Spock.
Yum yum yum.

See Nurse Chapel duck.

Duck, Nurse Chapel, duck!

Spock does not want any soup.

See Yeoman Rand.

Yeoman Rand has a lot to do.

Yeoman Rand must attend
to the Captain.

Yeoman Rand must take
sensor readings.

Yeoman Rand must spend
hours getting her hair done.

See the crewman.

   What is the crewman's
   name?

   It does not matter

   Why does it not matter?

   He is wearing a
   red shirt.

      It is best not to get
   too attached.

Uhura had one Tribble.

Now she has many Tribbles.

Tribbles are here!

Tribbles are there!

Tribbles are everywhere!

Tribbles are trouble.

See Sulu's sword.

Sulu's sword sure is sharp!

Sulu's sword goes swish!

Swish swish swish!

Sulu sheathes his sword.

Sulu's sword is safe and sound.

See Abraham Lincoln.

Hello, Mr. President!

See Uhura.

Hello, Lieutenant!

See Abraham Lincoln see Uhura.

What did you just say, Mr. President?

See Uhura diffuse the situation with grace.

See Spock.

Spock wants to get information from the alien.

Spock will use a Vulcan mind-meld to get the information.

See Scotty.

Scotty wants Spock's attention.

Scotty is worried about the warp engines overheating.

Spock is distracted and accidentally
uses a Vulcan nerve pinch.

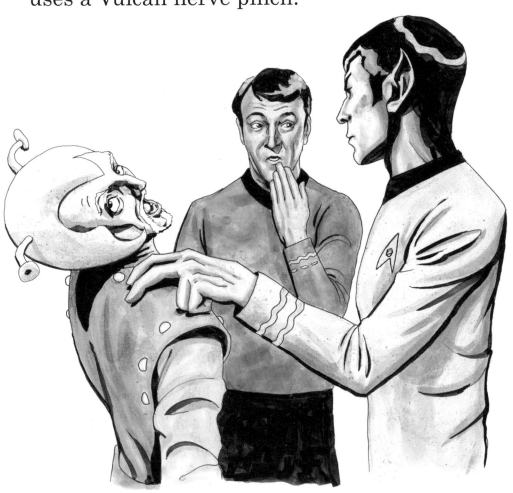

Oops!

Will you run with us, Spock?

"No, it is not logical."

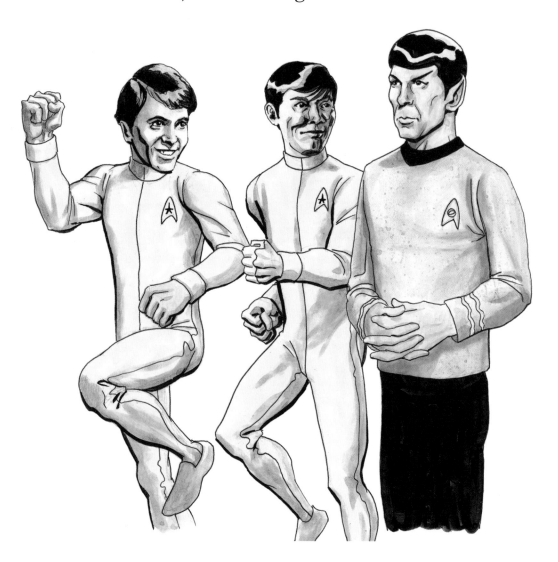

Will you climb with us, Spock?

"No, it is not logical."

Will you swim with us, Spock?

"No, it is not logical."

Sometimes Spock is no fun.

Scotty loves Carolyn.

Apollo loves Carolyn.

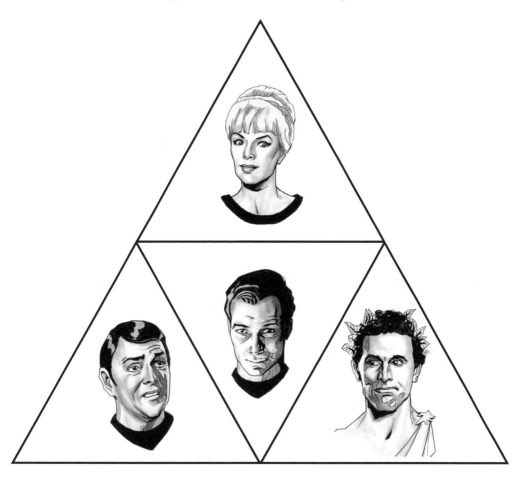

Carolyn loves them both in their own way.

Scotty and Apollo and Carolyn

are in a love triangle.

See Kirk win in the end.

Poor Captain Pike.

Captain Pike was in a terrible accident.

Captain Pike cannot walk.

Captain Pike cannot talk.

Captain Pike can get preferred parking spots.

See Spock mutiny.

"Why, Spock, why?"

Kirk wants the truth.

Spock does not think Kirk can handle the truth.

See Spock take two episodes and use the unaired pilot to explain his actions.

See Chekov.

See Chekov beam down to the planet.

See Chekov follow orders.

"Go here, Chekov!" says Kirk.

"Go there, Chekov!" says Spock.

"Stay put, Laddy!" says Scotty.

See Chekov talk about Russia.

Let's meet Spock's parents!

See Spock's mother. Her name is Amanda.

She is Human.

Hello, Amanda!

See Spock's father. His name is Sarek.

He is Vulcan.

Live long and prosper, Ambassador Sarek.

Spock is bi-racial.

Let's visit Bones in Sick Bay.

Why are you in Sick Bay, Bones?

"I'm a doctor!"

Sulu has a scratch. Ouch!

See Bones scan Sulu.

Kirk has a cold. Achoo!

See Bones scan Kirk.

See Spock come in with a problem.

See Bones call Dr. M'Benga in for a consult.

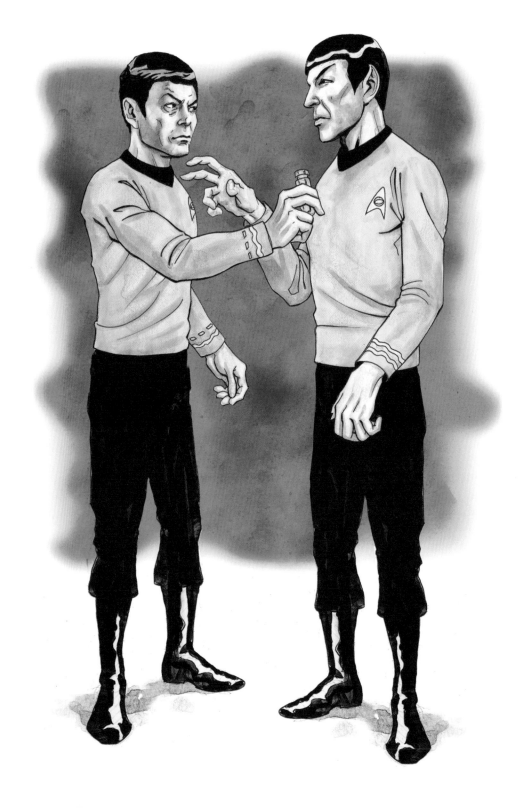

See Bones.

Bones calls Spock a pointed-ear hobgoblin.

See Spock.

Spock calls Bones illogical.

Spock and Bones help each other.

Spock and Bones are worried about Kirk.

Spock and Bones are frenemies.

See Bones.

Bones is upset.

Kirk wants Bones to help the Horta.

"I'm a doctor, not a bricklayer!" Bones says.

But Bones helps the Horta.

Bones is pleased with himself.

See the Gorn.

The Gorn is tall.

The Gorn is green.

The Gorn is wearing a one-piece sleeveless tunic with brocaded accents and matching gauntlets.

The Gorn is fashion-forward.

Shhh.

Everyone is asleep on the *Botany Bay*!
Tip toe Tip toe Tip toe.

See Khan wake up.

Khan is cranky.

Khan wants to take over
the *Enterprise*.
Mine! Mine! Mine!
Khan wants to take over
the universe.
Mine! Mine! Mine!
Khan is not a morning person.

Look, Kirk! A box from Tantalus!

What is in the box?

What is in the box from Tantalus?

Is it a promotion for Spock?

No, it is not a promotion. Spock assumes
only temporary command.

Surprise!

It is Doctor van Gelder, a violent
and rambling escapee!

Hello, Doctor van Gelder, hello!

See Trelane.

Trelane wants to play with the crew
of the *Enterprise*.

Trelane thinks the crew of the *Enterprise*
are his toys.

Trelane is rough with his toys.

Trelane wants them to play piano, dance,
and die.

Trelane's parents put a stop to his foolishness.

See the *Enterprise* map star patterns.
Something is blocking the way.
It is a spinning cube:
Spin, spin, spin!

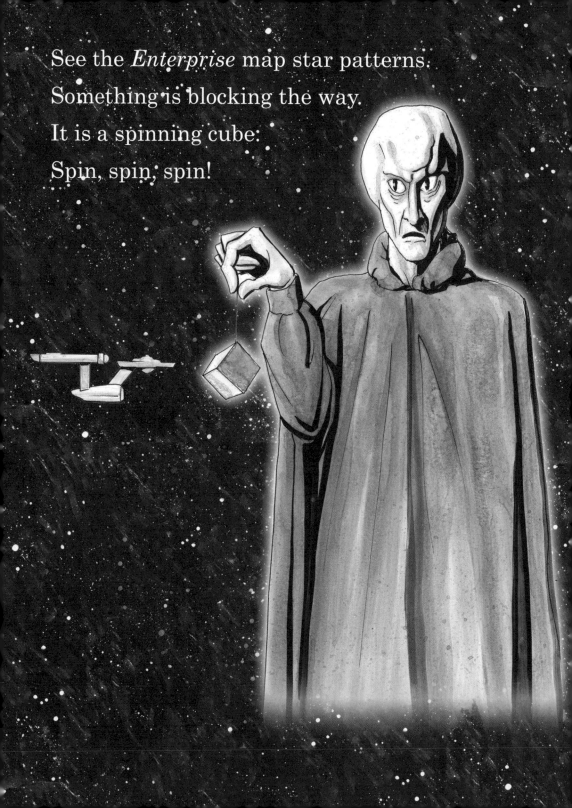

See Balok, the hostile alien.

Balok is cruel. Balok is threatening.

Balok is—...*that's* Balok?

Oh.

Kirk and Uhura and Scotty and Bones beam up to the *Enterprise*.
Up Up Up Up!
It is a different *Enterprise*.
This *Enterprise* is in a parallel universe.
It is a bad universe!

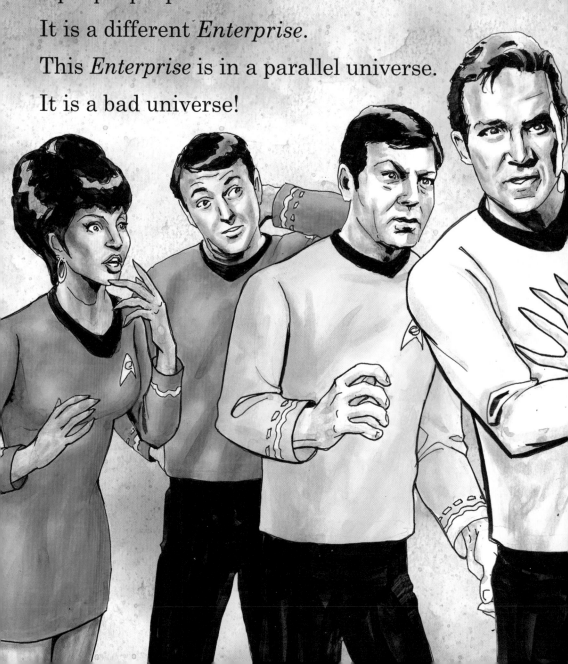

In this universe, Spock has a beard.
In this universe, Kirk refuses
the advances of a woman.
This is a bad universe!

Hey you. You see 'dis here, pal?
You see Kirk?
Kirk here sees a society stuck
in 'da 1920s.
'Da Boss, Oxmyx, he's lookin'
for heaters, see?
Lottsa heaters.
'Da boss wants heaters t'take
out Krako, see??
'Dis here's what happens when
ya violate the Prime Directive.

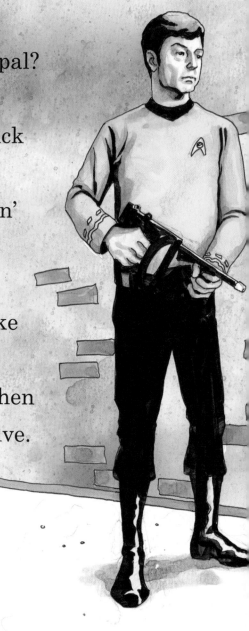

See Lokai. Lokai is half white and half black.

See Bele. Bele is half black and half white.

They are different.

They are the same.

They are doomed.

See Flint.

Flint is very old.

Flint has seen empires grow.

Up up up.

Flint has seen the fall of civilizations.

Down down down.

Flint has seen thousands of years

come and go.

Go go go.

Flint sees his android companion Rayna

develop feelings of love for Kirk.

Now Flint has seen everything!

The Klingons are on
their way to Organia.
Zap Zap Zap.
Organians know when Kirk
and Spock have arrived.
"Hello, hello, hello!"

Organians know when
the Klingons have arrived.
"Hello, hello, hello!"
Organians know their
planet is important because
Organians know the first
rule of real estate:
Location. Location. Location.

About Cider Mill Press

Good ideas ripen with time. From seed to harvest, Cider Mill
Press brings fine reading, information, and entertainment
together between the covers of its creatively crafted books.
Our Cider Mill bears fruit twice a year, publishing
a new crop of titles each spring and fall.

"Where Good Books Are Ready for Press"

501 Nelson Place
Nashville, Tennessee 37214

cidermillpress.com